Books for young readers by Robert Coles

DEAD END SCHOOL

THE GRASS PIPE

SAVING FACE

SAVING FACE

SAVING FACE

ROBERT COLES

ILLUSTRATED BY ROBERT LOWE

An Atlantic Monthly Press Book
Little, Brown and Company   BOSTON   TORONTO

LIBRARY OF CONGRESS CATALOG CARD NO. 79-170853

FIRST EDITION
T 04/72

ATLANTIC—LITTLE, BROWN BOOKS
ARE PUBLISHED BY
LITTLE, BROWN AND COMPANY
IN ASSOCIATION WITH
THE ATLANTIC MONTHLY PRESS

Published simultaneously in Canada
by Little, Brown & Company (Canada) Limited

PRINTED IN THE UNITED STATES OF AMERICA

Again for Bobby and Danny;
now for Michael, too;
and once more for their mother

SAVING FACE

I

EVERYBODY knows who the police are. You look at a policeman and wonder where his billy club is, or his gun. All that shows is his uniform and his badge. Maybe he *is* wearing his belt and his holster, and inside his holster the gun is there, right where you can see it. Then you wonder if he's ever used it, and what happened when he did.

My dad is one of them; he's a policeman. He's in line to be promoted, and pretty soon we won't be calling him a policeman or a cop; he'll be a sergeant, a police sergeant. He'll get his stripes and he'll have a desk and there'll be a sign on it that says Sergeant Paul J. Reynolds. He may live to be a lieutenant, and then he'll have to go and give speeches to businessmen, he says, and things like that. He might even make enough money so we can live better. But don't bet on it, he says, because the

3

police don't get the pay they deserve. None of them do.

We get by, our family does. Dad does a little moonlighting on the side. He has to. All his buddies on the force do. The Chief of Police says they mustn't, but he knows. A policeman doesn't make a lot of money. All he does is protect everyone! If he didn't do his work, everything would fall apart. That's what my social studies teacher told us. My dad said it was true except that no one gives a damn for the cop. Pay him? No one wants to pay him much of anything! People just want him to do his work. Then they can forget about the police.

With his job at the warehouse, Dad does O.K. He mostly sits and rests there. He sleeps some. He's supposed to guard the place and open it up for the trucks that come and make sure the lights are off, that nothing goes wrong with the heat, and all that. Once I went with him and he showed me around. I've never seen so much stuff in my life. Now I know where the supermarket stores things. They keep millions and millions of cans of soup and jars of jam in that warehouse and my dad walks all over the place, to make sure no one has broken in to steal something. Every once in a while he wonders what it must be like to be on the other side—trying to break in and cause trouble, instead of trying to prevent trouble.

Dad says today there are more crooks than ever before. He's been with the police for a long time, since before I was born. He should know. He says people want everything easy. They'll steal to get what they want, or they'll freeload. Dad says the world is full of freeloaders. They don't work. They get paid for sitting at home and doing nothing. The city gives them a check. They are people who should be working, but they don't. They only pretend to look for jobs. My dad has two jobs.

Once he was almost killed. My dad was walking down the street and a guy came running out of a store. He ordered the guy to drop what he had in his hands. The man pulled a knife and almost got him. People just stood there, and it was a good thing my father could get to his gun in time and stick it in the guy's ribs. He begged Dad to let him go. He said he didn't have any money and he had

5

hungry kids at home. Dad said he asked the man why didn't he try to work for a change, but the man didn't answer and he was sent to jail by the judge.

My mother is very proud of my father. Maybe he isn't rich, but he's doing a big job, she says. My father laughs when he hears that. "What you're telling them is that the cops protect the big boys, but they don't get rich doing it."

That gets my mother going. "How can you expect your children to have respect for you if you talk like that? You're a *policeman,* not a cop, and you're as important as anyone in the city," she says. Then my father will laugh and say he'll remind her of that the next time she asks for a new toaster or a washing machine. He jokes and says he'll let my sister, Marjorie, come around with him when she gets bigger, but not us. We might get ideas, and the next thing he'd know, we'd be wearing the uniform, like him. And he doesn't want that.

Marjorie is his pet. She's everyone's pet. She's five, and she has some trouble. They think she was hurt when she was born, but they don't really know, the doctors. They told us she was a slow child. She'll

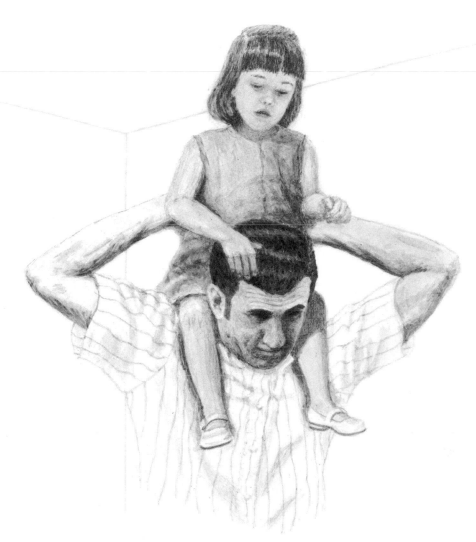

always be a little retarded, but it won't be so bad
that she'll be funny, you know. I mean, she can talk
and dress and take care of herself all right. It's just
that she can't learn as fast as most kids, and she'll

have to go to a special school next year. Dad loves her. Mom does, too, but Dad does especially. She's pretty and she waits all day for him to come home. He waited and waited for a girl, and finally she came.

There are three of us boys. There's my big brother Paul, Paul junior, he's sixteen. There's my brother David. He's thirteen. And then comes me. I'm Andy, Andrew J. (for James) Reynolds, and I'm ten, nearly eleven. My birthday and Marjie's are almost on the same day in March. I was born on the fifth, and she on the seventh. Marjie won't go to the same school my brothers went to, the one I'm at now. With all the trouble we've had at our school, she may be the luckiest of the Reynolds kids, that's what my dad says.

We've been having a lot of trouble. This is the second year of it, but the trouble in school is just the beginning. According to my dad, everything is going wrong in America now, and he says we might as well know right now, us kids, that when we grow up we won't be able to live the way we want without someone ordering us around. Dad says it's bad enough fighting criminals without a lot of people trying to destroy the police and push everyone around so that the whole country won't be the same anymore.

Last year they brought some colored kids to our school. They said we were supposed to have them, because we didn't have any, and if you don't have any it's wrong. My dad thought it was the stupidest thing he'd ever heard of. So did everyone on our street. Me and my friends were lucky, though. They didn't try to send us to another school. They took some kids who live on other streets away from our school and sent them over to the niggers. But not us.

"Don't use the word 'nigger,'" my mother shouts at us. "It's not what you should call them." My dad says, "Hell, that's what they are." He's tired of them, he says. And he's tired of college students. He says that it used to be that the police kept cars from speeding, and made sure robbers got caught, and things like that. Now there's one riot after another. The colored people and college kids, they're always rioting or complaining about something.

No colored people live on this street, or the others I ride my bike on. But they're moving closer. A lot of them want to leave their own streets and come out here. That's how the school got into the trouble. The colored said they wanted their kids with us kids; we said no. We said if you don't live here, why should you go to school here? They said they wanted us all mixed up, the colored kids and us. That's what my dad explained to us. He said we were going to have to take some of it, the colored kids in school, but there's just so far they can push us, he said. And they'd better know that, he said, the school people and everyone else had better know it.

"It's in the courts," my dad keeps telling my older brothers. He says you've got to wait until the judges decide, and until then there's nothing we can do, except let the school board know we're not happy with all their games. One minute my father says the law is the law and you've got to respect it. The next minute he says the time may be coming when people will have to stop letting themselves be pushed around and told to do this and do that and give up this and give up that.

"It's always us," Dad says. "It's always people like us that are told they've got to save the country. No one's pushing nigger-kids into rich towns. No one's taking *rich* kids and sending them to fight our wars." He gets angrier and angrier. He punches one hand into the other, and my mother tells him to stop, but that gets him going even more.

My cousin Tim is in Vietnam, and Dad talks about him all the time. He wishes the world had more Tims and less college demonstrators.

Demonstrators, we hear a lot about them. Dad has to fight them, to prevent them from getting everything they want. They're ready to march all over the city. They call him every name they can think of. Mom tries to tell Dad that they'll grow out of it.

"They'll grow out of it. Sure they will!" he says. "They'll grow out of it by becoming worse, much worse. They're revolutionaries now. They'll try to take over the whole country soon, if we don't stop them. And their pets, do you know who they are? The niggers are their pets."

My mother tells him to stop talking like that. He shouldn't let the demonstrators get him so worked up. "Sure it's unfair, the way people take the police for granted. Your father and most of the police in every city don't get the money they should, and everyone expects them to do miracles for practically nothing. The police are taken for granted, all day and all night they are. But even so, you can't lower your standards. It's not right to think ill of people, to be prejudiced. The Negro people are poor, and they've been treated very bad for a long time, and that explains why they have all these demands. They want to be equal with the rest of the people."

My mother doesn't back down when Dad gets angry. She's very religious. (That's what Dad says, and he says that's why she talks like she does.) She tells us what she heard in church, in case we weren't paying attention to the priest. My father goes to church with us, and he's not against the church. But he'll sometimes say that it's O.K. for priests and ministers to talk so nice and be so kind to everyone. But if they saw what he does in his work, then they'd talk a different line.

"They've got it made," according to Dad. "They can preach and preach at us about love and equality. They side with the college professors and their hippie students. But it's families like the ones around here that keep this country going. If there weren't people like us, there'd be no factories turning out cars, and no police and no firemen and no carpenters and no plumbers and no one installing telephones. Then where in hell would we be?"

When Dad cools down, he tells us he hopes that the three of us boys *move on up.* "Move on up. Get out of this setup if you can. Get an education. It's no picnic being a policeman, let me tell you, Andy."

I told him I wanted to be a policeman, just like him. My mother shook her head. She said I'd do better if I became a lawyer. My dad said that was a good kind of job to have. Then he gave me a long lecture. "If you're a lawyer, people will listen to you," he said. "If you're a cop or a mechanic in a factory, or a carpenter, like my brother, or if you work in a store, something like that, no one pays any attention to you. They just push you around. They *take* from you. They take your taxes and you can't afford a big, fancy accountant to help you get around the government and hold on to your money. They draft your sons, like they did Tim. They force the colored people down your throat, whether you like it or not."

My mother tried to stop him but he waved both his arms at her and went right on. "And then, if you so much as raise your voice, you're told that you're not being very intelligent and you're prejudiced, and why don't you go and be generous. That's what they preach at you—be generous. But who is being so generous to *us*? If we had dark skin, they'd be here handing out welfare checks and patting us on the back, the government and the college crowd and the rich ones out in the suburbs. But all we are is white people, working people, plain ordinary Americans. That's all!"

When the trouble started at the schools, Dad was so upset he almost quit the force. He talked about moving us out to Wyoming or Montana, where we wouldn't be going through all this. "If we could afford it. You have to know someone out there, or have some money to tide you over until you get work." I guess he was only dreaming.

I can close my eyes and see what happened that day they brought the colored kids here. It was last year, but so much has happened since then that it seems like a hundred years ago. A few of us were standing near the door of the school when all of a sudden one of those small buses stopped and out came about ten kids. "They're colored. They're colored and they're here," one kid shouted.

The colored kids were walking so fast they practically were on top of us in a few seconds. You could almost feel those kids go by, and after they'd gone inside we just stood there not saying a word.

Then a teacher came up to us. "You're all pretty quiet," she said. "Times change." Before we had a chance to say anything, she'd gone inside so we shrugged our shoulders and started inside ourselves.

Suddenly we heard a siren, and then another one —and before we knew what happened the street was covered with police cars. In a few seconds the kids and teachers who'd gone inside were back outside.

We all stood around, and it was funny how quiet it was. We wondered about the police until five or six cars pulled up near the school. They were full of people who lived nearby. They could have walked, but they drove instead. They got out of their cars and started walking back and forth in front of the building. There were more women than men, and they carried signs that said NO BUSSING.

Then the police got out of their cars, and there he was. My dad was standing in front of the Frank C. Crawford School. That was the first time I'd ever seen my dad at the school in his uniform. We've driven by on Sundays, on our way to church, and seen him standing near the school, but that's different. This time he was pushing people away, including some of our neighbors, and he was mad.

"Keep off the school property," he kept on saying.

Mrs. McNeill, who lives a block from the school, kept asking why, why? "Isn't this my property?"

My father said yes, it is, but he was under orders to keep the crowd from interfering with the children going to school. Mrs. McNeill said that she just wanted to look, not interfere with anything. She just wanted people to know how she felt about the niggers in her school.

"Please, Mrs. McNeill," my dad said, and I guess she understood him, because she moved back and started telling all the others to move away. "The police are in a tough spot. They need all the help they can get," she kept saying.

Later Dad told me he went over to thank Mrs. McNeill, and she said that she never admired anyone more than she did my father. He had the worst job in the city, protecting the school because of the mistakes the school board made, even though he knew it was wrong, what was happening.

We didn't want the colored kids, but we hardly even saw them that first day. Someone said he saw all the colored kids going in and out of the principal's office, and we heard they were kept in the library most of the day.

Miss Brooks explained what had happened. A

judge had ordered the school board to "re-draw the lines" so that some colored kids would be with us. While she talked I remembered that my dad said the best of the colored, the really good ones, don't want to come to school with us any more than they want us going to school with them. It's a lot of busybodies who cause the trouble, people from outside the city who don't have to live with the trouble they cause.

I was there real early the next morning. "Everything will be quiet and O.K.," my dad told me. "People get excited on the first day and they quiet down on the second day." He was right, as usual. First our buses came. I walk to school, so I was just there, standing and watching. Then theirs came, the one bus with them in it. They got out and they didn't look to the left or the right. They just marched in without looking at anything. They *must* have been curious. Someone must have told them to pay no attention to anyone, just walk toward the building. I overheard a teacher (he was watching, like me) say that they were like little toy machines that had been wound up and put down on the floor.

Three of them were in my class. Mostly we ignored them and they ignored us. Miss Brooks spread them all over, one in the front row, one in the middle row, and one to the back of the class. Then something happened. Someone tripped Kenneth Wilson, the smallest of them, and he started to cry, and he wouldn't stop, and when he did, he was still shaking. I felt sorry for him. So did the teacher.

"Who did that?" she shouted at us. I'd never heard Miss Brooks talk like that, so loud. No one raised his hand. Then she kept on shouting. "I've known this class since September, for two months. No one has ever tripped anyone. Now suddenly Kenneth is tripped, and he's frightened. He's only been with us a week and it's been a bad week. You've been snickering and smirking and whispering and behaving very poorly. I didn't want this change any more than anyone else but I'll not have rudeness in my class! You hear? You'd better!"

I told my parents about it when I got home. My mother felt bad, the way I did. She said it was hard on them, the colored kids. My dad said yes, he agreed. But then he said that no one was forcing

Kenneth Wilson to come to our school, except his own mother and father. "If they wanted to keep him in his old school, they could have. They could have told their neighbors to stop agitating, and they could have told their friends out in suburbia to mind their own business and stop trying to mess everyone else's life up."

That was just the beginning for Dad. He got red in the face, like he does, and finally Mom had to start shouting, too. She shouted that he should stop shouting.

Anyway, after they finished arguing, they told me to stay out of trouble and not trip anyone or be mean to anyone. They switch back and forth when they talk with us about school. Sometimes my mother gets mad, because she thinks the school can't do a good job anymore, because of the colored kids. Then my father will say that "no one can prevent you from learning, if you really want to learn." I think my mother is afraid that the school won't be so good, and then I'll be like my brother David.

David doesn't care about school at all. He's in the eighth grade, and he says he doesn't want to stay in school after he's sixteen. But he'll have to because Dad won't let him do anything until he graduates from high school. Then he'll go into the marines, David says he will. He loves to play baseball, and he's the track star of the junior high. He's like a sports car. He starts going, and he goes and goes and goes, faster and faster, until you think he's going to take off and fly. They've brought in a lot of colored kids to the junior high, too, and David is faster than them. They're good at sports, and they usually can run faster than white people can.

David was telling us how one guy asked him if he didn't have some black blood in him, because he ran "like a black man." Dad asked David what he answered and David said he tried to be real cool and say "maybe, maybe." When David said that, Dad dropped his fork. "What do you mean?" he shouted at David.

"He's teasing you," Mom said.

The one who gets my father maddest, and my mother, too, is Pauley. He's the oldest. From kindergarten on, as Mom says, it's been like this: "Pauley is as smart as David is fast. Pauley will be the first in our family to go to college." Dad has an insurance policy that will be paid up when Pauley is eighteen. He gets two thousand dollars. They took it out when Pauley was a baby and now Dad says it's not worth much, because everything is so expensive, especially college. But Pauley will get a scholarship, the teachers say. He says he wants to be a doctor, something like that, but my parents say you have to be rich to send your kid to school for almost ten years, and a policeman can't afford it.

Pauley is always changing his mind. Once he thought he'd try law. He even thought he might be a teacher. "*Don't* be a teacher!" my mother said.

"Your mother is one hundred percent right!" my father said. "You'll end up in the same boat I'm in. You'll half starve to death."

Then Pauley said he didn't want to go to college just so he could make a lot of money. My mother said people should do what they like doing, but you've got to have money to pay your bills. My father said he'd change his mind, Pauley would, when he got older. And look what's happening to the schools.

Pauley said he didn't see any teachers going to jail. Dad said, "No, not yet. The only teachers who go to jail so far are the ones who are always demonstrating, and *trying* to go to jail, so they can brag about it. It's a great honor with some of them, you know, to be pulled into a police van and driven off."

Then Pauley had to make it worse by saying he was glad they were bringing colored kids into my school. There have always been some in his school, the high school—though a lot drop out after a year or so. Pauley says they're as good as anyone.

"Hell, who disagrees with that?" my dad asked him.

"Well, I think you do, Dad."

Dad got red and leaped up from his chair. Then he looked at my mother and sat down again. He emptied his beer can and my mother shook her head. She answered Pauley, instead of Dad. "We have taught you children that everyone is born equal. God doesn't prefer one child to another. Some children are smarter than others. Some races are better suited to one kind of work than another.

You're smarter than Marjie, Pauley, but that doesn't mean you're *better* than her. You're both equal. Before God, you're both equal."

Pauley nodded. Dad said, "That's right!" Then she went on.

"All your father and I think is that there's a difference between colored people and us—between the colored kids that come to Andy's school and Andy and his friends. They have different values. They talk differently. They believe in different things. You can see it when you drive through their neighborhood—the way they live. Now, why should different people have to live near each other or go to school together? It will only make *all* the children suffer. They'll be having such trouble with each other that they'll sour on school."

Pauley laughed. He said Mom was being silly, and she was exaggerating. Dad said Pauley was the one who was being silly—and stupid, too. Dad said he wanted Pauley to go to college real bad, but he was getting more and more scared that Pauley was going to "get lost" there. "You'll start thinking like those crazy, damn college freaks I have to haul before the judge. You'll be wanting to change this and change that. And I'll end up having to bail out my own son! That will be the day!"

Pauley laughed; so did Dad. He was only half-serious. He keeps on telling Pauley that he has a "level head" on him, and he'll be O.K. Pauley says he doesn't really care that much about politics, anyway, or the colored people or what they're trying to do. "Keep it that way," Dad says. "Politics is for the rich and the very poor," he says.

I remember last year I thought my father was going to die right before my eyes. He came home and he just stood there in the hall. He couldn't seem to move or talk. Suddenly he asked me to get him some water. I brought him the water and he just held the glass in his hand, but didn't drink from it. He began saying what he does, about politics being for the rich and the colored, but he was whispering.

Suddenly he told me to call the doctor. He was afraid he was getting a heart attack. He sat on the chair we have in the hall, and kept rubbing his chest with his left hand and holding on to the chair with his right. I was all alone with him and I got scared. I ran to the phone and was going to shout to the operator to send a doctor over, but Dad shouted to me, "Hang up."

I must have been slow to obey him, because he practically screamed at me to hang up. So, I did.

I went over to him and he seemed better. He got up and moved to the living room and sat down on the sofa and drank the water in one gulp and asked me for more. I brought him three glasses in a row, and finally he was filled up. I asked him if his pain was better, and he said yes. I could see he was O.K. He began to stretch his legs and he stopped rubbing his chest and he looked better, not so pale.

"Don't ever be a cop," he told me. I'd heard him say that a hundred times. When he's really tired and fed up he says that. Then he told me how he'd spent the afternoon fighting with demonstrators, and they'd called him a pig and other words, and stuck their signs in his face and someone threw a rock that almost hit him in the head.

I said that some people are lousy and no good. Just as I finished, Pauley and my mother came into the house, and sat down and asked what was going on.

"Nothing," Dad said.

They all looked at me, and I didn't want to disagree with Dad, so I didn't say anything. Then Dad exploded, and I mean exploded. His face got red and he started to wave his hands while he talked and then he picked up the ashtray as if he were going to throw it at the people he was telling us about. "The rich can afford to go messing around and get arrested and put up bail and all the rest. If they lose their jobs, so what? They can live off their stocks and bonds. And they have friends. They know the judges. They know the people who own the newspapers and write for them. Hell, I'm no fool. I see those people parading and demonstrating, and they'll say hello to the reporters and call them by their first names, you know? They're putting on a production, that's what it is. You have to be a fool not to see that. The demonstrators call up the newspapers and the television people and tell them they're marching.

"They started by calling us 'pigs,' and a lot worse

28

than that. Then the stupid news media people, the reporters and camera people, they came rushing over and building it all up. If we went near those demonstrators and so much as told them to move on, they shouted louder. They were screaming 'pigs' and 'police brutality.' And tomorrow you read about it in the paper. It will be *us*, the police, who are wrong! Us!"

Dad was going on and on until Pauley interrupted. "O.K., Dad, O.K. I know, I know."

Then Mother interrupted Pauley. "Let Dad finish his point." She's always telling us to make our point, and to finish our point.

Dad did finish. He said it's easy to protest or become involved in "causes" if you're rich. "But if you're a workingman you have to worry about losing your job or being arrested, and you have no money to fall back on. If you're poor," he said, "you just *have* to go and stand up for yourself, because no one else will, and you've got everything to gain and nothing to lose, anyway."

Then Pauley yelled, "Aren't Negroes poor? Aren't they?"

Dad flew off the handle again at that one: "Hell, yes; but because they don't go and work. A lot of them are lazy—lazy, period. They prefer welfare checks, free money, to work. I know. I've patrolled those districts where they all live. You don't know the half of it. No one in this house does."

He got up and paced back and forth. He loosened his belt and then he tightened it and we all knew we'd better keep quiet. When Dad is really mad, *that* mad, it's best to shut up and disappear. I was just ready to slip out of the room and go find my friends when *he* left. He said, "Hell!" and walked out. He went down to the cellar.

He goes down there and makes furniture—chairs or tables. Once he showed me all his tools, and promised that when I get bigger he'd teach me how to build a desk for myself.

I can remember one day he was standing there in front of his bench and smiling and talking to Pauley and David and me. David and I like to watch him working with his saw and plane, measuring things very carefully. He whistles and sings to himself while he works and he's proud of what he makes.

He takes a Coke with him and sips on it. He starts out by drawing a picture of what he's going to build, and then he buys the lumber, and begins.

He'll let me help him sometimes. He almost always pats me on the back and tells me I'm doing a good job. David and I both like Dad best when he's in that shop of his, working away. And Dad says that sometimes he'll be at the police station and a tough job comes up, and he'll wish he was back home building something, and not having to go patrolling and looking for people who have broken the law.

Dad's brother, my cousin Tim's father, is a carpenter, and he was the one who taught Dad how to build things. Dad tells us it's better to be a carpenter than a policeman, but people step over *all* "hard-working men," which means both my dad and my uncle. When he starts on that track he leaves the bench and goes upstairs and we stay down there. Dad's a tough man but I like him. He's really good to us. He's the one who taught me how to play baseball, and he got David running. He's always helping with Marjorie, playing with her and holding her and making her laugh. He really loves her and it's tough for him. He used to sit with Pauley and help him with his schoolwork, too.

Sometimes I show Marjie the pictures in a book, and I try to tell her what they're about, but she can't keep it in her mind very long. A lot of what you tell her never registers, and Mom gets mad at me when I try to explain things to Marjie. She says Marjie is Marjie, and why am I trying to turn her into a big brain? Well, I'm not. Mom and Dad have got to stop protecting her, always protecting her.

"Let the kids take Marjie and show her how they play," Pauley tells Mom. "Let her have a life on the street, with other kids." But my mother's eyes will fill up, and then Pauley backs down and Dad will talk real low and sad but fast.

"Don't push Marjie into water over her head, you hear? She's not one of you guys and she's slow. If you can't think of the right things to do with her, then don't do anything with her. Leave her alone, just leave her alone. We'll take care of her and see that she has a happy time for herself."

Then Dad will get up and go down to his bench in the cellar, and the next thing you hear is the saw going back and forth, or the hammer going. Or he'll go and work on the lawn, like when he told me to stop trying to teach Marjie to ride my old bicycle. I told him I'd just finished cutting the grass. It was O.K., and didn't need any cutting. "Any more advice, Mr. smart-aleck Professor?" he said to me, and he went right on pushing the old mower.

2

BACK IN SEPTEMBER, at the beginning of this school year, they brought some more colored kids into our school. In my class we had seven, and they weren't like the three last year. Mr. Burke is not as easy-going as Miss Brooks was. He wants silence in the room. *"Silence!"* he yelled once or twice every hour. And did he make us work! He would send us *home* with work. My mother wondered why. She said I was too young for homework but my dad said good, good that we were being pushed to learn. And I didn't mind it. I liked a little reading after baseball. I would come in tired from playing, and my mother would bring me a tall glass of water and a Coke and I'd drink both of them down and sit and read the history book and get ready for Mr. Burke's questions the next day.

Dad says Mr. Burke should be a professor. He

says Mr. Burke has a good head on his shoulders. He's not crazy like a lot of college professors are. Pauley had Mr. Burke, but that was a few years ago. Pauley didn't like him much, and now Pauley says he never heard Dad praise Mr. Burke *then*, when he taught Pauley. Pauley says Dad likes Mr. Burke because of what he did. Ever since then, last October it was, Dad has talked and talked about Mr. Burke—and I guess everybody else in the neighborhood has, too.

I was right there in the room when it happened. I was in on it. My brother Pauley tells me I should try to forget what happened. My dad says: Never forget, because I'll probably see worse, and I should be prepared. It started when one of the colored kids, a boy named Arthur, said he hadn't done his homework. Arthur was frightened and said he was sorry. Mr. Burke didn't seem to feel sorry for Arthur. I did. He looked tired, and I thought he might be sick. He was leaning hard on his desk while he stood there and said, "I couldn't do any work last night."

"Why?" asked Mr. Burke, and he was angry, you

36

could tell by the way he was tapping his ruler on the desk.

Arthur didn't answer. He coughed, though, and you could hear a funny noise in his chest. I was sure the kid was sick. He'd always been quiet and friendly and I'd thought he was the easiest going of the colored kids we had in our room. I expected Mr. Burke to ask him if he was feeling O.K., and send him to the school doctor. Instead he got angrier and angrier. He glared at Arthur, stopped tapping his ruler, and for a second we sat there and you could have heard dust fall in that room. Then: *Wham,* Mr. Burke got up, threw his ruler down on his desk, and raising his voice so you could hear it on the other side of the city he said, "Arthur, what is the capital of Pennsylvania?"

No answer.

Mr. Burke stood there and stood there. I got nervous looking at him. He was staring up at the ceiling, so I looked up there, too. All I could see were some spots and cracks.

Then Arthur coughed again, and I *knew* he was sick. He shook when he coughed and I thought he was going to double over and fall down. But he didn't. Instead he cleared his throat and surprised us all by coming up with an answer: "Philadelphia."

"No. That's wrong. That's wrong."

Arthur started to sit down, but Mr. Burke told him no—"Stay standing."

Then he really started giving Arthur a lecture: "If you want to come to a school like this, you can't be lazy. No one asked you to come here, but now that you're here, you've got to do your work. Philadelphia is *not* the capital of Pennsylvania. Understand?"

He was going to say more, but suddenly Arthur coughed again. Then he mumbled something. I didn't hear what he mumbled, and neither did Mr. Burke. All I could see was that the kid wasn't feeling good.

"Arthur, repeat what you just said, so that the class can hear it."

Arthur said nothing, and I thought to myself, I wouldn't do any different. I'd just stand there and hold my lips tight together.

"Arthur, tell the class what you just said."

Well, Arthur didn't say a word. So, Mr. Burke moved nearer and nearer to Arthur and Arthur just looked right at him. I expected him to lower his head and stare at the desk or the floor, but instead he stared right up at him, at Mr. Burke.

"We're waiting," Mr. Burke said. Still not a word came out of Arthur's mouth. I got more nervous inside. I was scared. I thought Mr. Burke was going to pull Arthur away from his seat and pin him against the blackboard or something. I guess Arthur's friend Thomas must have felt just like I did, because all of a sudden he shouted out to Mr. Burke, "You leave him alone! You leave him alone!"

Mr. Burke whirled around fast. I can remember thinking to myself that he did it like a cowboy does, real fast. If he'd had two guns on him he could have pulled them out in a second and had them trained on Thomas. He walked over to Thomas, and came right up to his desk, and pulled him up out of his chair and pushed him with his pointer to the front of the room. Thomas was scared. We all were. I didn't know what would happen next. I sat there, on the edge of my seat. Then all of a sudden Arthur screamed out, "Keep your dirty white hands off him. Don't you touch him! Don't you!"

Mr. Burke must have stood still for only a minute or so, but I thought it was an hour. What's he going to do, what's he going to do, I kept on thinking. Finally he told Thomas to go sit down. Thomas did, fast. Then Mr. Burke went back to Arthur, and picked him up, like he had Thomas, and started pushing him toward the door. But Arthur wouldn't let him do it. He pushed back with his body, back at Mr. Burke's hands, which were on Arthur's shoulders. Mr. Burke kept pushing, and Arthur kept pushing back, and somehow, I don't know what happened, Arthur fell down. Mr. Burke seemed surprised, but before he could do anything Arthur was up and running, and in a flash he was out of the room.

Mr. Burke didn't seem to know what to do next. Then Thomas got up and started for the door. Mr. Burke told him to take his seat, *immediately*. Thomas didn't. For a second he stood there, halfway to the door. Then slowly he turned around and walked back toward his desk. All of a sudden, he changed his mind and ran to the window. He stood there, sort of shaking and watching for something.

Richey, who sits next to me, looked at me and shrugged his shoulders. He didn't understand. "He's looking to see if Arthur is out there," I whispered to him. I wondered where he would go. He doesn't live *that* near here. The colored come here by bus. Does he know his way home? Would he dare just leave and go home like that? What would his mother think? He'd really get into trouble.

I don't know how long Thomas stood there. Mr. Burke didn't try to make him sit down. He didn't do anything at all. We just sat there in dead silence. You could hear the clock moving its hands. We must have heard it two or three times, that clock. Usually you never hear it, except at the end of the day, when you're waiting to be let go. We all watched it. We didn't know where else to look. Even Mr. Burke was looking up at the clock. He must have been thinking about what he should do, just as we were wondering what *he* would do.

Then he lost his temper. Suddenly he was scrambling up from his desk and was over by the window, pulling Thomas back toward his seat. Thomas screamed, "I want to see Arthur. I want to go with him."

A colored girl stood up and spoke very quietly,

almost crying. "Please, Thomas, sit down and be quiet. Please." Her name is Lucy, and she's a quiet one. Then I thought about all those other colored kids in the room and how they'd been watching all of this, just like me. There was Thomas, and her, Lucy. And then we had four more, a girl whose name—it's a strange one—I always forget, and Lois, and two more boys, George and Willie.

Richey and I were staring at Mr. Burke. We all were staring at him. Mr. Burke let go of Thomas and just stood there. Thomas kept his eyes glued to his desk. I kept looking at the other colored kids, the girl with the funny name, at Lois and Lucy, and then at George and Willie. They were staring at Thomas and Mr. Burke.

Then it was over. Mr. Burke went back to his desk and asked who *did* know the capital of Pennsylvania. We all raised our hands, all the white kids, and he called on Richey.

"Harrisburg," said Richey.

"Yes, that is *right*, and it's about time we got that answer!" Mr. Burke sounded relieved.

Richey smiled and sat down. And then we went

on with the other states, New Jersey and Delaware, and their capitals, and what their big industries are, and the seaports and rivers and all that. We were beginning to forget about Arthur and Thomas and the trouble.

By the end of the day, we were ready to go home. I had almost forgotten about Arthur. But Thomas still was scared. He'd been sitting at his desk, bent over and not moving at all. Mr. Burke had called on him once in the afternoon and he answered the question right away, but he stuttered, the first time I'd ever heard him do it, and he sat down so fast we all looked at him. He didn't look back, just stared down at his desk.

When I got home, I told my mother and father all about what happened. My mother kept on saying, "Terrible, terrible," the way she does.

When I was all done talking, my dad said, "What can you expect?" I waited for him to go on, but he didn't. Then Mom asked him if he thought Arthur would be back the next day. "Yes, of course." Dad seemed to be more interested in his paper, so I left the room to go watch TV.

Just before the six o'clock news, I went out to the kitchen to make myself a peanut butter sandwich. Dad was there reading the paper at the table and Mom was cooking. I had eaten half my sandwich when David came rushing out.

"A kid from your school, a colored kid, claims he was knocked down and insulted by a teacher—Mr. Burke! His parents and all their friends say they're coming to the school tomorrow and they won't leave until they get an apology from him and from the principal. They say Mr. Burke should be fired, or transferred to some other school where there are no colored kids."

I thought David was fooling. I thought he'd heard me telling the story to Mom, and now he was trying to kid me. I said, "Cut it out." He said, "I'm not kidding you." I said, "Sure, sure." He said, go and call up the TV station. I could tell, then, that he wasn't kidding.

Dad was up and out of the kitchen in a flash, switching the TV from one channel to another. The news was over except for sports and weather, so he called up the police station. Sure enough, the lieutenant had heard the news, and he'd been warned, by main headquarters to have all his men ready the next morning in case there was trouble at school. They might need the police; they might even need reinforcements from all over the city.

When Dad put down the phone he was excited. He called Mom and she came out of the kitchen. "How do you like that?" Dad told us. Pauley came from his studying to listen—just in time to say, "Like what?" Dad asked me to tell the story, and I tried, but he kept interrupting.

"The damn niggers," he kept on repeating. He didn't want to hear any more about Arthur. He didn't feel sorry for Thomas. Instead he told us that the colored people are lazy and they collect more welfare checks than any other group in America. Pauley was itching to fight with him on that, but Pauley knows when to shut up and let Dad talk. I wanted to speak up. I wanted Dad to know that Arthur was just a quiet kid, and Mr. Burke had pushed him too hard.

"Hell, a day doesn't go by that I don't catch one of them, kids like Arthur, no older than you, Andy, stealing an old lady's pocketbook or pushing drugs or trying to shoplift. They're crooks. So help me they are! They want everything for nothing."

Pauley started to say something, but I guess he decided to keep quiet. Dad just went on and on. "And you know who's right in there with them? The answer is: the civil rights crowd, the college types, with long beards and crazy clothes, always calling me and others 'pigs.' And that's not the half of it. They say they want peace, and they want the colored to have more, but has anyone heard the filth that comes out of their mouths, those holier-than-thou people?"

Mom's lips were thin. She knew she couldn't stop Dad. "And now, you just wait and see tomorrow," Dad yelled. "They're going to come over to your school, Andy, and they'll have a couple of ministers with them—they always do. White flunkies, we call them, the ministers and the college weirdos. They'll all be shouting at the principal and his teachers. They'll be shouting at everyone in this neighborhood, calling us *racists*. That's the magic word: *racists*. If you're a policeman you get two words:

racist pig. And the reporters and TV cameras will be there, hanging onto every single word. The police get telephone calls and letters from plain, ordinary people, wanting to know why all the crime, why all the riots and demonstrations. Do the papers pay attention to the people who write those letters? No, because they're sitting there at home, not parading up and down the streets with signs in their hands and filthy words on their tongues."

That's when Pauley interrupted him. All he said was, "Dad!" I could feel myself getting ready to say "Dad" too—but I didn't want to argue with my father, like Pauley does. I couldn't say it, but I knew that Arthur and Thomas were right and Mr. Burke was wrong. Mr. Burke was mean to them, meaner than he's ever been to us *white* kids. I wanted to speak, but I couldn't.

"Don't you *Dad* me, Pauley. You don't know. You're in school. I'm out on the streets. You have to see to believe." But Pauley wasn't going to stop.

"You're unfair, Dad. You're talking about colored people as if they were all alike, and you're talking the same way about college students. Would you

like it if I said the police were all a bunch of bullies and crooks? Would you like it if I said all cops take bribes and beat people up? You used to tell me when I was a kid, when I was Andy's age, that there are some *mean cops*. Those were your words. I remember. You'd say to me: Don't ever be a cop, son. You said that the police aren't paid enough, and they're always in danger of getting killed, and they're tempted to collect bribes and kick people in the pants for getting in their way. You said that.

You told me that you had to fight with yourself to stay clean and be nice to people."

"You shut up!" Dad roared. "Don't go and twist my words. My own son—a big shot, a brain. You aren't going to be one of those. Oh, they're good at saying this and saying that, until you're dizzy just listening to them. They'll go over to Africa or Asia to study a tribe or something, and they'll bend over backwards to understand *them*. But do they ever try to understand how the rest of us people in America feel? Do they care about the ordinary workingman? No. They're snobs, that's what they are. And let me tell you, Pauley, you get your education, but if you get full of their fancy talk, you'll kill your mother and me. I'd rather see you collecting garbage. I swear I would."

Then my mother grabbed his arm. "Stop, both of you. Let's wait and see what happens tomorrow. We're jumping the gun. Maybe that boy—what was his name, Arthur?—will just come to school and somehow they'll settle it. I know Mr. Carter. He's a good man, a good principal. He was the one I went to see about Marjie. He told us about that school for her. He's a gentleman. He'll know how to handle the colored. Probably the boy went home and told his parents all kinds of crazy things. Kids get excited. The boy's parents will bring him to school and Mr. Burke will talk with them, and Mr. Carter will, and it will all settle down."

Dad knew she was wrong. He kept on shaking his head while she talked. He stood up, but he sat right down again. He must have felt like I do sometimes in school. I want to stand up and talk—you know, just say something—but I can't. Then Marjie came into the room. She had spilled a bottle of shampoo all over the bathroom. It hadn't broken, lucky for her. Mom went out to see about the mess.

Mother never raises her voice at Marjie. Sometimes I think she's really ruining her. If Pauley or David or I try to tell Marjie she's done something wrong, *anything* wrong, she cries. Then Mom comes out and shouts at us. She says we're wrong, we're wrong. *We're wrong!* How can you beat that? No one has ever told her she's made a single mistake! In her whole life no one has!

I know she's slow. I feel sorry for her. We love her, all of us do. When I'm grown up, she can come and live with me. I once swore to my mother that I'd take care of her, for the rest of my life I would. And since I'm not so much older than she is, I'll be around as long as she is. My mother came over and hugged me. She didn't say anything except "thank you." But I saw that she was crying, and I couldn't get it out of my mind.

I told Pauley about it, because he's smart, real smart, and he understands what's going on. I wish I could be as smart as Pauley. Or as good at basketball, too. He's tall, and he just *puts* the ball in. He doesn't have to throw it, I swear. He stretches himself and places it right in that net, and the next thing you know everyone is cheering his head off.

Anyway, after I told Pauley about Marjie and what I said and what Mom said, and her crying, he told me that I had to remember that Marjie was like someone who is sick, and she needs more attention, only she won't get better. Well, I know it. I've known it ever since I can remember. But do you help Marjie to give in all the time, and never say no to her about anything? I asked Pauley, and he said, "Of course not." Then he changed the subject.

I remembered all that when Marjie spilled the shampoo. As soon as Mom saw what Marjie had done she came back to us, yelling that if we hadn't been doing so much talking, Marjie wouldn't have made that mess. Dad went to help clean up and he said it goes to show that the more you talk about politics, the more trouble you get into.

Then Pauley got mad. It wasn't fair, the way they blamed *us* whenever Marjie did something wrong. He didn't want to blame Marjie, but he didn't feel we should blame ourselves. He started pacing around the room, and went to the phone and tried his friend Eddie, but Eddie wasn't home. He came back and asked David and me if we wanted to hit a few balls out in the yard.

Yes. We both said yes and we practically ran outside, the three of us. We started taking turns hitting and catching. Then David said he'd race us. He gave Pauley a half a block lead and me a whole block, and beat us both to the main street, which is two blocks from our house. David is an airplane. He's a jet airplane. He says it's because he eats Wheaties. Pauley tells him to come off it, and stop talking like an idiot. No one believes a breakfast cereal makes you a fast runner, but David says he's superstitious. Every good athlete has to be, he says. His superstition is Wheaties. "Wheaties is a healthy superstition, and an inexpensive one," Dad always says, so David gets his Wheaties every morning.

Mom called us to supper. We could tell she was upset. She didn't smile and she went right back in. When we came and sat down I could tell that there was trouble. Mom hung over Marjie, asking her to eat, and telling her what books she and Dad would read to her before bed. Dad didn't say anything. When Pauley asked him if he'd heard more about the trouble at school, he said, "Enough of that," and we all knew better than to go on and say anything else.

I hate to see my father like that. Feeling "down in the dumps," he calls it. He doesn't talk. He sits and stares, or he plays with Marjie. It's as if he's not paying much attention to her, just doing something to keep himself busy.

After supper he snapped out of his mood. All of a sudden he really turned against us. "The way you three acted before supper was terrible. You hurt your mother. You ganged up on your little sister. She has enough troubles in this world without hearing from you three big lugs that she shouldn't do this and she shouldn't do that, and her mother is spoiling her and all that. I'd like to see you boys, any of you, take care of yourself as good as Marjie does, considering what she's up against."

Pauley half opened his mouth, but then he walked away. David turned on the television and I joined him, but we didn't say a word to each other all the rest of the evening.

▮▮

THE NEXT DAY was some day! I'll never forget what happened. It was the middle of the week, a Wednesday. Dad was on the phone when I came to breakfast. I drank my orange juice and started in on the cereal. When he put the phone back on its hook he sat down and looked at his cereal. He didn't look at me.

"I'm taking you to school today."

I said, "You are? What's happening?"

"Five or six of us cops have kids there in your school, and we might just as well show up with our kids. Then we can head off trouble if there is any. We're parents of kids in the school, so we can speak up loud and clear if they show up."

"Who do you expect to show up, Dad?"

"There's no telling. Maybe no one, which is usually what happens after they start making threats. I mean, they don't follow through. But they could turn up with an army of civil rights people, just looking for trouble."

"An army," I said, and I could see in my mind the whole school yard filled with colored people, all screaming at Mr. Burke.

"I'm talking about maybe twenty or twenty-five colored people, and they'll bring along their white buddies—*and* some TV cameras."

I began to get excited while Dad chewed on his toast and drank his coffee. We could really have a time there in school, watching people march up and down and watching the television cameras click away, and all that. Maybe they'd close school! Maybe it would take a week or a month to settle the fight! And I started wondering whether Arthur would show up. And would Thomas? I was pretty sure the rest of them would—the other colored kids.

Well, with all that talking and thinking, we were late. Mom yelled at us and grabbed my jacket and pushed my lunch into my hands and kissed me fast and sort of brushed me out of the house. Dad was running ahead of me, as if he wanted to go out on his own, without Mom hurrying him up.

We climbed into the car and in a few seconds we were out of the garage and on our way. In a couple of minutes, we were in sight of the school, and after all our talk, it looked just like it does every day. I thought to myself, *nothing,* nothing at all is going on there. And I'll be truthful, I was disappointed. I was looking forward to a little noise, a little excitement. School is so slow; it can be a real bore a lot of the time, like Pauley says. We sit there and sit there and Mr. Burke calls on us every once in a while, and in between he has us writing down a lot of stuff that I forget two minutes later. I'd really looked forward to a lot of action and maybe they'd take pictures and I could see myself on television. Instead, there it was, that same old school, with a few kids walking toward it and a bus parked there.

But my father had sharper eyes than I did. "Look, Andy, there's a squad car." And there it was, parked right behind the bus. The red light on the roof was going round and round. I asked Dad if that meant that there was trouble. "No, not necessarily. But when I put my light on while my car is standing like that, I'm telling everyone in sight that we're ready, we're all set."

I started feeling better. I thought maybe something special would go on, and I could see us all pushing on one another so we could look out the window. That would mean no reading for Mr. Burke and none of his questions about what is the capital of Rhode Island or New Jersey. Then I remembered it all started that way, just because Mr. Burke asked Arthur the capital of Pennsylvania and Arthur didn't know the right answer. Then for some reason Dad decided to stop the car about a block from the school, and just sit there.

"Do you want me to walk the rest of the way?"

"No, no. Just sit here for a minute. I want to wait and see what happens when the colored bus comes."

I couldn't resist being smart. "All the buses are the same color, Dad, yellow and black."

"Come on, Andy. Use your head. What's the matter with you?"

He turned on the radio, and pushed one button after another. He was listening for news, and as soon as he heard music he frowned, or said "damn it" and pushed again. Then he turned off the engine and pulled up the emergency brake. He decided we needed a little heat in the car so he started the engine up again and we got the heat right away, because the car was warmed up. I thought of asking Dad some questions—about what he'd do if a lot of colored people suddenly came. But he was staring out at that patrol car, and waiting.

All of a sudden Dad said, "There she comes." It was the bus with the colored kids.

"How did you know so fast it's the colored kids on that bus?"

"I have good eyes. It's one of the requirements for a good cop, Andy. He has to have perfect vision. He has to be able to spot trouble before it gets out of hand. He has to scan a neighborhood as if he had a microscope and a telescope and a searchlight in the back of his head."

He kept staring at the bus. Now I could see the faces of the kids. I mean, I couldn't make out exactly who they were, but I could see they weren't white, but were colored. And the driver—he's colored—I could see him turning the big wheel and looking out the window for traffic, and pulling the bus to the curb.

The kids came off the bus, one after the other. I was watching for Arthur and Thomas, but we were too far away. Dad moved our car nearer, all the time keeping an eye on the bus. "Do me a favor. If that kid Arthur shows up, tell me. Point him out. I want to know if he comes and what he looks like."

"O.K., Dad." We stopped and parked across the street from the bus and the police car. I watched every one of the kids get off—but no Arthur and no Thomas, either.

When no one else came down the steps the driver closed the door. I turned to Dad, but before I could say anything *he* told *me*: "He wasn't on the bus, was he?"

"No, Dad, he wasn't, and neither was Thomas."

"Thomas? Who's Thomas?"

"He's the kid who shouted at Mr. Burke. He told

Mr. Burke to leave Arthur alone. And he was worried about what happened to Arthur. He's a friend of Arthur's and he's not a bad kid."

That slipped out, what I said about Thomas being O.K. Dad didn't seem to hear me. He was too busy watching the school. All he said was, "He didn't show up either?"

"No, Dad."

"Well, that does it. We're going to have a bit of trouble here today. I give it about a half an hour, no more."

He buttoned his coat and then he took the car keys and put them in his pocket. "Let's go, Andy."

"Dad, can I stay with you?"

"Until school starts, and then you'd better go inside."

"Dad . . ." I guess he knew what I was about to say because he took hold of my shoulder the way he does sometimes, and gave me one of his "friendly little lectures," he calls them. "Look, school's important. It won't be long before you're grown up, and all the rotten troubles of the world will be on your shoulders, like they are on mine. Now, you go in there, Andy, and you show Mr. Burke how smart you are."

He looked right into my eyes, and I knew he wasn't going to change his mind and let me stay with him. He checked his watch just as the school bell rang—the bell which meant that everyone was supposed to be in his room and in his seat. I'd never heard that bell before from the outside, and I was surprised that it was so loud you could hear it across the street. Dad told me that "enough is enough," and I should go in right away, and if Mr. Burke asks where I was, why I was late, tell him my father kept me longer that he should have, with his talking. We crossed the street, and Dad did let me walk with him over to the police car.

"Hello, Paul. Is that your youngest boy?"

"Yes, Ted. Andy, this is Ted Dutton. Ted and I were rookies together. We've gone through a lot together."

My dad and his friend looked worried, I could see. They stepped away from me and talked, though I couldn't hear them. I saw my father listening while Mr. Dutton talked, louder and louder, until he was almost yelling. "Just let them try something," Mr. Dutton said. "They'll regret ever coming here if they don't watch out." I was scared for a minute. Even Dad seemed a little nervous. "Take it easy, take it easy," he told Mr. Dutton.

Finally they stopped talking, and Mr. Dutton smiled at me, and then I asked him a question. "What do you think, Mr. Dutton—will there be trouble?"

"We're ready," said Dad, and his friend nodded and said, "You bet we are."

I suddenly caught myself blurting, "Arthur isn't a bad kid. Neither is Thomas. They were scared yesterday. That's all. They're probably still scared."

Mr. Dutton said, "Yeah?" I could tell he didn't believe me. I also knew that Dad didn't like the way his friend spoke to me. Dad told me to go inside. I didn't move fast enough, because he repeated himself, and I *knew* he was serious.

"I said it's time to go into that building. You'll

soon see a mob of people coming down the street. It'll be part of your education. You'll learn what the world is like."

I was glad, real glad, to say good-bye and walk into the building. Mr. Dutton acted as if he wanted trouble. I almost spoke up and said that Arthur and Thomas only wanted to be left alone, but I didn't. I really felt like Pauley did. I felt my dad was wrong. I wished he and Mr. Dutton could have been there, in Mr. Burke's room, and seen what I'd seen and heard what I'd heard. I thought to myself: Dad is on Mr. Burke's side and I am on Arthur's side and Thomas' side.

When I came into the room late Mr. Burke gave me a funny look, but he didn't say anything. I just went to my seat.

Mr. Burke was doing the spelling. He'd say a word, then call on one of us, and we had to spell it, or if we didn't do it right, the next person he called would have to try with the same word. Usually he sits at his desk and looks at his list of words. This time he kept walking back and forth, between his desk and the windows. He carried the list with him, and when he got to the window he stared out at the street.

I knew he was staring at the police car. I could tell because he'd asked a kid—Betty, who sits two seats behind me—to spell *hospital*, and she did. She stood and spoke the word and spelled it and then spoke it again, the way he wants us to, and then she waited for a second or two, for him to say right or wrong. When he didn't say anything, she sat down. We all sat there waiting. Then he came to his senses and he said, "Betty, have you spelled hospital yet?" She said yes. He said, "O.K., that's fine." His eyes were still looking outside to the street when all of a sudden the principal, Mr. Carter, came into the room. It was 9:30; I know because Mr. Burke and Mr. Carter both looked up at the clock. We all looked.

They moved toward the door and faced away from us so we couldn't hear what they were saying. They were worried. Then they both quickly walked over to the window and looked out, and kept looking, but not talking to each other. I felt like running over and looking myself. I could hardly keep myself in my seat. I even got up and took a step down the aisle, but I went back when the kids nearby looked at me as if I were acting real strange. I was itching to say something, too. I wanted to go and tell them, the teacher and the principal, that I knew what they were worried about, and not to worry, because the police knew—my dad and his friend Mr. Dutton, and others—and they could handle things.

They stood there a minute before the principal turned around and ran out of the room. He ran, that's right. Mr. Burke walked back to his desk and leaned on it, but didn't sit down. He seemed lost in some thought. Then he walked back to the window fast, and looked out again, and scratched his head, and looked at us, and then he said, "I'll be damned." Once Thomas, I think it was, used "damned" about something he was describing in a composition, an "oral composition" they're called, and Mr. Burke nearly murdered him. "Don't *ever* use that word again—or any others you may have on your mind. Not here. Not in this room. You hear?" Now Mr. Burke was swearing, and he looked scared. He started straightening his tie. He looked at his watch.

He looked at the clock on the wall. And he cleared his throat a couple of times—but he didn't say a word.

Then the school bell rang. It wasn't supposed to ring until noon, when we start going to the cafeteria for lunch. I knew there was trouble outside. I just did. There had to be. And sure enough, Mr. Burke started shouting orders to us. "Everyone clear his desk! Get ready to form a line! We will be going to the cafeteria. There may be a little trouble out in the street, but it's nothing to worry about. Mr. Carter just wants to talk to us. It will be better if we keep away from the windows for a little while—until it's all cleared up outside."

He knew we had a million questions, and he made a funny smile. "Don't worry. Mr. Carter will explain everything to you, to us all." Then he left the room to see if the other classes were out in the hall and ready to go, or just getting ready, like us. ("Teachers are like kids," Pauley once told me. "They're always worried about what the next guy is doing.")

I couldn't stop myself, now that Mr. Burke was

gone. I knew he could come back any second, and I'd get caught and I'd hear it from him, I'd hear plenty! But I decided it was worth it. I ran over there to the windows because I *had to run*, and nothing in the world could stop me. I had to know what was going on. I guess I knew more than the other kids, too much to just sit there and imagine all kinds of things happening outside.

There must have been a hundred colored people out there. I saw Arthur and Thomas. There were grown-ups and high school kids, about Pauley's age, I guess. They were waving signs, and yelling, though I couldn't make out what. And there wasn't just one police car. There were five of them, I counted. And just like my father had said there would be, there was a big truck, with cables all around it, and on a platform sticking out of the back of the truck was a camera, a TV camera. Everything Dad said was right. Everything was coming true, everything! And I couldn't stop looking, even though I knew Mr. Burke would soon be stepping back into the room, and there I'd be, and he'd really tell me off. But I couldn't do anything—except stay right where I was and look and look. The police were in the middle of the crowd, so it was hard to see them. Then I saw a uniform and I saw my dad. I was so excited I must have said out loud what I thought I was saying to myself. "There he is, there he is!"

"*Who* is there?" said Mr. Burke's voice. He was standing right behind me.

I turned around and stared at Mr. Burke. He just stood there. He stood there, and I could feel him breathing. Finally he turned around and pointed to my seat. I got the message fast.

And suddenly I knew Mr. Burke was scared, *really* scared. I saw the police cars and the TV and the colored people, all of them. And Mr. Burke, he saw them, too. He must have seen Arthur there, and Thomas. He was afraid they would point him out, and their parents and friends would get him because of what he said yesterday.

That's what I was thinking as we filed out, row by row, to the hall and then marched to the cafeteria. By the time we got there I'd told most of what I'd seen and guessed to Richey. And all he had time to say was, "Wow!" Then as we sat down in the cafeteria Richey whispered, "I'll bet Mr. Burke never expected *this* when he left for school this morning."

Mr. Carter said he didn't want to speak very long, but he did have something important to tell us. "This school is being picketed today. There are people outside who have complaints about us. I don't want to go into what they say and what our teachers and I say. I simply want to tell all of you children that there isn't much I can do to stop what is happening outside. It may be that we all will have to go home. I have been told that a number of the men and women marching outside plan to come inside the building. I hope just a few of them will come in, and that I can have a quiet talk with them. But if things get too loud and bothersome, I won't hesitate to ring the bell three times, which means get ready to go home. The school buses will arrive, and we'll ring the bell three more times, which will mean form lines and march to the street just as if it were the end of the school day. I am sorry about all this, sorry for the children and the teachers of this school. But I do believe that this trouble will soon pass, and then our school will be able to do what every good school does, help children learn—and nothing else!"

He was angry. He raised his voice at the end, when he said "and nothing else!" He nodded to several teachers and they told us to get up and go back to our rooms. They were all shaking Mr. Carter's hand, and I heard Mr. Burke say, "Thank you, thank you," as he and the principal talked and kept on shaking hands. The teachers were scared, anyone could tell that, but trying to keep cool. They were more scared than any of the kids. The first and second graders didn't even know what was happening. A few of them cried and wanted to go home. They could tell there was something wrong, but they didn't know what. I kept on wishing I was outside with my father. As it was, I told Richey that I probably knew more about the trouble than anyone else, because my dad had told me what would happen the night before. Richey said, "You sure know what's going on, don't you? I wish my dad were a cop. He never knows what's happening."

"I'm lucky. Dad's in on a lot of things other people don't know about."

We got back to the room and Mr. Burke tried his best to pretend nothing was wrong. We did some reading. He showed us a movie about the Eskimos and how they live in igloos and catch seals and eat them. He read from the history book—the chapter on the War of 1812, between the British and us. But we could tell where his mind was. He'd lose his place reading or ask the same question twice. And while we were watching the Eskimo film he was staring out the window. Even when he read to us he walked toward the window and kept stealing looks outside, in between sentences. I wasn't hearing much of what he read, because I was trying to imagine what he was seeing out in the street.

Just before lunchtime, Mr. Carter opened the door and cleared his throat. Mr. Burke almost ran to the door, and then he listened while the principal whispered to him. I wished I were sitting closer, so I could hear what they were saying. Then Mr. Burke told us that he had to leave the room and go to the principal's office. We should be quiet, and take out

74

our history books and read. He said Miss Knowlton would be looking in on us from next door, and so we'd *better* be quiet.

Mr. Carter was standing just outside the door tapping with his foot, while Mr. Burke was talking to us, telling us to be quiet and all that. As he was leaving his desk Mr. Burke said, right out loud, "All right, all right, I'm coming." He was talking to Mr. Carter and he was annoyed; we could tell by his voice. He was mad at being ordered around by Mr. Carter.

Teachers are always ordering *us* around, saying do this, do that, and now's the time for something and now's the time for something else. If you try to ask them a question or if you let them know you don't agree with what they're saying, they jump on you and call you "disobedient." That's what Mr. Burke calls us all the time. Well, now *he* was disobedient for a change, and I told Richey maybe it'll do him good to hear Mr. Carter telling him to step on it.

He was gone about a minute. We just had time to think about his being "disobedient," like he calls us, when we heard a lot of noise in the hall. The voices were loud and angry. I couldn't sit in my seat any longer. I wanted to go out into the hall and I wanted to run to the window and I even thought of leaving the building to see if my dad was out there in the street.

The noise in the hall got louder and louder. There were a lot of people out there. Then I heard some shouting. Richey and I both ran to the door, along with other kids—our whole class, I guess. There was Miss Knowlton, standing just outside the door. She was too busy looking at what was happening to do more than glance at us and say, "Don't push, just stand where you are."

Then they came, the colored people. They had signs that said FIRE THE RACIST TEACHERS. And they were shouting the same words. "Fire the racist teachers."

Richey looked at me and I looked at him and we both said at almost the same second, "Mr. Burke."

Miss Knowlton heard us and said, "No, it's not true."

Then the police came. I looked for Dad. He wasn't in the hall. There were only four policemen, and they had their sticks out. One of them stepped in front of a big woman who carried the biggest sign. "You are trespassing on city property. Get out." Everyone quieted down, and the cop looked very red.

"Arrest us. We're not going," the woman said very slowly and almost whispering.

I counted fifteen women, all colored, and two white men. One man with glasses was very tall and had on a gray suit and a white collar, so he was a minister. The other one looked not much older than Pauley and he had a sign that said JUSTICE FOR ALL. I couldn't understand that one. One of the kids asked Miss Knowlton what that meant, and she said, "Nothing, it's silly." Then she added, "We have always had justice for everyone in this country. That's what America is all about."

The people kept moving down the hall, the colored people and the white men, and the police followed them. Then Mr. Carter came out of his office, and Mr. Burke was beside him. By this time Richey and I had moved out into the hall.

"That's him. That's the racist teacher," one

woman shouted. Mr. Carter held up his hand and everyone was shouting and waving signs around. Then Mr. Carter walked over to the policemen and said something. The police moved toward the colored people and then started shoving a couple of them toward the door to the street. The two white men moved fast toward the police and the minister said, "No, we shall not leave. We want to stay here and tell the teachers and the children of this school that there is a better way, a loving way, for people to behave." Then he just sat down on the floor, and so did his friend, the other white man. The colored women all sat down, too.

One of the policemen raised his billy club and let it swing from his wrist. The other three stood over the people sitting there, but didn't touch them. Mr. Carter and Mr. Burke were mad. Mr. Carter's face was all red, and he was sweating and wiping his forehead with a handkerchief and pacing up and down in front of his office. Mr. Burke was standing still, holding himself up against the wall, and glaring at the people sitting there. He didn't move, not an inch. They started singing some song about "We

Shall Overcome," and they repeated it over and over again. Mr. Burke suddenly walked away and so did Mr. Carter. They both went into Mr. Carter's office.

The people kept on singing and the police just stood there. Then one of them went into Mr. Carter's office, too. Richey said he bet we'd get let out of school. I said, "No, I'll bet they call in more policemen, and they get those people out of the school."

Then Richey laughed. "They'd have to get twenty cops at least."

"Well, there are hundreds of cops, thousands of them!"

Everyone was staring at the colored people in the hall. The little kids were bunched up together and were quieter than they usually are. A few of them said "Go away," or "Leave us alone." Some of the kids in the fourth and fifth grades were smiling, but you could tell they were worried, too. And the teachers—they were almost trying to ignore the colored people and their signs, even though they were right there in front of us. They kept on telling the children to stay away, go back into their rooms, and keep out of the hall. One teacher said, "It's all right; nothing's wrong." Yeah, yeah, I thought to myself.

I wanted to see what was going on *outside*. So, I pushed my way back toward our room and went to the windows. There must have been a hundred police cars out there, including the *chief's* car, the Chief of Police. I looked and looked—and I'd never seen so many policemen except in a parade. Then I saw my father leaning up against a car and talking to another policeman. He was smiling as if he had heard a joke. Then he was laughing, and the other man was waving his hands and enjoying the story he was telling my father, I could see that.

Then it happened. A policeman, I guess the same one who'd gone into Mr. Carter's office, came out of the school building and went over to the Chief of Police, who was sitting inside his car. I could see only his shoulder and his arm with all the gold braid, but then the chief's whole head came out of the car window. He listened to the policeman talk.

Then he stuck his head inside. Maybe he was listening to something on the radio or getting news on the special phone he has.

Richey came over and leaned his elbows on the windowsill. "What do you think, Andy?"

"They're deciding. They're deciding now, that's what I think. There's my father." I pointed to him.

"He's laughing, isn't he? You think they're going to do something funny? You think they'll try to fool the colored people out there in the hall?"

"Of course not, stupid," I said to Richey. "My dad just likes to laugh sometimes."

Then my dad stopped laughing and moved toward our school building. The police all lined up, like *we* do when we're getting ready to go someplace—to the lunchroom—and they started marching in the front door of the school. I kept my eyes on my dad. I wanted to run and meet him and be with him, but I was afraid to do that. I knew he wouldn't like it. Once my brother David got into a big fight, and he came home and asked Dad to go arrest the guys. He said he wouldn't even if he could, and he couldn't. And he said he never wanted to be mixed up in something that had to do with his family. Maybe that's why I saw him look up at the building just before he went through the door. I could tell he was looking to see if I might be looking out the window. I waved to him, but it all happened too fast. He was in the door before I could open the window and shout to him.

I've never seen so much happen so fast. I ran from the window to the hall, where Miss Knowlton was still standing, along with all the kids—kids from her class and all of us in Mr. Burke's class. She was talking as if she were teaching, only outside in the hall and not in her room.

"This is what happens sometimes. People begin to take the law into their own hands. This is a country founded so that all people can be free. But you can't have freedom when people interfere with the rights of others. How can we have a school here, while all this is going on?"

Richey said to me, "Listen to her! Is she talking to us or herself or those people over there sitting on the floor?"

"To herself," I said.

"She's an old witch, anyway," I heard one of the kids say, and I looked around to see who it was—and it was a colored kid from Miss Knowlton's class. Then I began to wonder what they were thinking, all the colored kids. They must have felt real funny about all that was going on. Maybe they were scared, or maybe they were mad. I felt sorry for them, with their mothers sitting there on the floor and the police looking down at them.

It was the most exciting day I've ever had at school. Like Richey said, "It beats a movie." Police and more police came toward the colored people. I saw my father, but I didn't dare shout to him. Mr. Carter came over and told Miss Knowlton to get us back into the rooms. Then he turned around and went along with the police, back toward his office door. I guess Miss Knowlton was so curious herself, she forgot to obey orders. She stayed there and so did we all.

While Mr. Carter stood there with his hand on the doorknob, the police started dragging them out, one after the other. The women screamed "Freedom!" as they were pulled along by the police, and one of them shouted, "Mr. Burke is a racist!" Then they all chanted together, "Burke must go." It took about two policemen to each colored lady, and with each of the two men they needed a third policeman to shove along from behind while two policemen pulled them from the front. My dad didn't pull any of them. One woman started kicking, and she cried and cried. The police stopped dragging her and she was lying right in front of me. She couldn't breathe and I thought she was going to die. She broke out in sweat, and she clutched her chest, yelling, "You're treating me like dirt. Just like you treated my boy."

I felt like crying—I felt scared and sick and sorry. I wanted to go over and be with her and tell her I was all for her and all for Arthur. And then Arthur came. He leaned over and hugged his mother and he told her she'd be O.K. He held on to her hands and kept talking to her, and she stood up with his arm around her. Some of what he said was in whispers, but then he'd raise his voice and we all could hear: "Let's get out of here, Momma. Let's leave. To hell with this school; to hell with the

lousy, crooked white people. All they've ever done
is beat on us. Now they're dragging on us. Let's go
and never come back."

They dragged out the last one, a fat lady she was,
crying out, "God save them from their hate!" I got

nervous hearing that. You begin to wonder about God. What must He think? They kept on singing songs as if they were in church while they sat there on the floor, and one of them shouted at the principal that Jesus Christ had been hated, too, and they killed Him a long time ago because of His ideas. I couldn't see what Mr. Carter or Mr. Burke did that was so hateful, though. Mr. Burke can be pretty tough on anyone, including me. But Arthur must have felt Mr. Burke was really out to get him. And Arthur's mother seemed like a good mother. You could tell she loved Arthur and he loved her. I couldn't forget the two of them, there on the floor. I looked at Dad once while Arthur was bent over his mother, and I thought he was maybe feeling sorry for them. At least he didn't look angry.

They did go. Arthur's mother stood up and she and Arthur walked out together. They had their arms around each other. Dad just stood there and stood there after the colored people were gone. He didn't smile or talk or even move much. He looked at the pictures on the bulletin board, that some first and second grade kids had drawn. Then he looked around, and I could see that he was wondering where I was, and how he'd get to see me. So, I lifted my hand up and waved it and waved it, but I was still afraid to yell "Dad!" He saw me and waved back. Richey and some others looked at me and him and knew without my telling them that he was my dad. I felt proud of him, standing there in his uniform, holding his nightstick. He was glad to see me, I could tell, but he looked funny. Maybe, I thought, he felt like I did—glad they got them out of the building, but sorry for them. They didn't seem like bad people, the kind the police arrest trying to hold up a bank or hit someone and beat him up, or something like that.

We all went back to our rooms. No one said anything. The only noise was our feet shuffling. Mr. Burke wasn't in the room, and Miss Knowlton couldn't be in both rooms at once, so she left us alone and stayed with her own class. We ran to the windows to see the colored people pulled down the steps and over the sidewalk. There were two police vans down there. The police got the people into them and off they all went, to jail I guess. And then the police went away, too—except for two cars and four policemen. The police weren't taking any chances. They figured more people might come, so they were going to guard us.

Finally Mr. Burke came back. We had left the windows and were in our seats, more or less, talking and kidding and horsing around. Richey and I were having a duel with our rulers. "We've had enough fighting for the day," Mr. Burke roared at us. He glared and we dropped the rulers. But he didn't seem in a very bad mood. He actually seemed happy. He smiled at Richey and me after we got to our seats. Then he gave us one of his lectures.

"I'm sorry for all this trouble we've had today. I wish it had never happened. But in a way I'm glad it all happened. You are young, ten years old, most of you. And you'll be meeting up with a lot more of what you've seen today. This country has had about as much demonstrating and rioting as it can take and keep going, that's my opinion. You're each entitled to your own opinion, of course, but I hope you'll go home and talk about what happened here with your parents and your brothers and sisters, and I hope you learn something from all this. Now we have work to do here, and I'm not going to talk anymore about all we've seen here today. Let's get on with our work and put the last couple of hours out of our minds."

That's about what he said, and that's what we did. You'd have thought nothing had happened. We did a little spelling. We went for our lunch—finally. We read in the afternoon. We did arithmetic. And we went home on time—and no one was outside except two, not four, policemen. Neither of them was my father, and I wondered where he was when I passed the two big men, standing there in front of the school. I wanted to go up and introduce myself as Paul Reynolds' son, but I didn't.

That night we sure did what Mr. Burke said we should do. As soon as I stepped into the house my mother came running up to me and kissed me. She doesn't usually do that when we come home from school. She kisses us when we go to bed, and in the morning before we go to school, if we're not rushing too fast.

"Are you all right, Andy?" she wanted to know.

"Sure, Mom, why wouldn't I be?"

Then she said why. "I was worried. Your father called me and told me what happened. He told me everything was settled, but still you never know what will happen these days. People get nasty. Mobs spring up out of nowhere. Buildings have been bombed. Oh, I shouldn't talk that way to you, but I was frightened, all day I was. Marjie could tell, too. She kept on asking me what was wrong. She's napping now. I hope she never has to go through what you did today!"

"It wasn't bad, Mom. It really wasn't. Honestly it wasn't. We all had a good time. We did! I've never seen so much *action* in school, never. It's too bad we don't have more days like today. This morning I didn't look at that clock once, not once. The first time I did was after lunch, when Mr. Burke was having us spell some more and read."

"I don't like the way you're talking, Andrew." (She always switches from Andy to Andrew when she's mad.) "Do you realize what *could* have happened over there at that school? Your father and you, the both of you could have been hurt. It seems a day doesn't go by that the papers and the television don't have stories of fights, protests, all of that kind of thing. Your father is right. The whole nation is being threatened by these people."

I didn't want to fight with her. I didn't even think she was wrong. It's just that I didn't really know what she meant. "But Mom, maybe Arthur really got scared by the way Mr. Burke came after him. He scares me sometimes. And Arthur hasn't been at the school very long, and he's probably nervous, like Thomas is. Then he went home and told his parents, and they got upset, like you and Dad do when we come home and tell you things—and well, that's what happened."

"No, that's *not* what happened, son." Then she told me to sit down and have a glass of milk and a cupcake. "It's one thing when you or Richey get scared of a teacher. I know Mr. Burke. All three of you have had him for the fifth grade, and he *can* be scary. But for a whole mob to come to the school and disrupt it and frighten so many children, that's

unheard of. Who do they think they are? The colored people have had a bad time, a real bad time. You've heard me say it, right to your father, even when it means an argument. But there's a limit. That's what I think. There's a limit. I hope those two boys stay at home, or go to a school near where they live. They could walk to school, then there'd be no Mr. Burke to bother them."

Mom stopped and poured herself more milk, and got a cupcake for herself. I was going to answer her. I was going to tell her she was wrong. But she started in again, and she was still upset.

"You can't win with the colored. In one breath they say they want to come and be with us, and go to our school. Then in the next breath they say they don't like our school and what we do, and they want to mess everything up and ruin the school. Why go looking for trouble? That's what I've been saying to myself all day. I'd like to go tell Arthur's mother *exactly that!*"

I shut up but I wondered what she'd have done if she'd seen Arthur's mother sitting on the floor at school.

After Dad and Pauley and David came home things got worse. I mean, Dad wanted to know how the rest of the day was at school, and Pauley and David wanted me to tell them everything. I did. I told them what went on. So did Dad. We talked and talked, and Dad said I would make a good newspaper reporter, because what I said was just the way it happened. Then we watched the news and there you could see everything—the school and the colored people and the police, just like I had told about it. We didn't see Dad. We didn't see any of us kids—just the colored people and the police who lifted them up and took them out. I thought they'd have Mr. Carter or Mr. Burke talking, but they didn't. They said that Arthur and his mother and Thomas and his aunt were hiring a lawyer, and they were going to sue the school people.

That's when Dad lost his temper, and that's when the big fight between him and Pauley got going. Dad couldn't get over the idea that Arthur's mother was going to sue the school board. "They have one hell of a nerve! They do illegal things, like marching without a permit and entering city property unlawfully and being disruptive, and refusing to obey a request to stop a demonstration. They insult the police, they threaten to 'close the school down.' And then, *and then,* they say they've been mistreated, and they're going to get a lawyer and go into the courts. Now what kind of a business is this? These people want *everything*. They want it both ways. They want to be able to disobey one law after another, because they claim they're not getting 'justice.' Then they use the laws whenever they please, to make others give them their way. And if someone disagrees with them, then he gets called every foul, rotten name in the book. I've been a policeman going on twenty years. I've never seen anything like it. We're in trouble. America is in trouble.''

Pauley has a way of lowering his head when he's getting ready to speak up to Dad. Dad was looking at him while he talked, maybe because he expected a fight. Then Pauley started. I can't remember the whole speech, but I'll never forget a few things he said. He kept repeating them. "A kid like Arthur isn't like us, like Andy. He's going to live a different life, and you know it, Dad. He'll be a nigger all his life. No matter what he's like inside, to others he'll just be what he looks like on the outside, a nigger. You call them the colored or niggers, and so do my friends in school—and so do I, yes I do, I'll admit. I see one of them doing something wrong, and the next thing I know I hear myself talking about 'the colored' or 'the nigger' and what he did, or he didn't do. We all laugh. We think it's funny. And the coach, the coach of our basketball team, *he* talks like that, too, even though two of our best players are Negroes, or black—that's what they call themselves."

Pauley didn't stop for one second to catch his breath, and Dad just sat there, tired. "I feel sorry for them, for black people," Pauley continued. "I'll bet they don't want pity from me or anyone else, though. You know how I know? I'm friends with one of the two black guys on the team. His name is Ed, Ed Jones. He's told me how he feels, and what it's like to live over there in the ghetto. He really does hate white people. He says he doesn't hate me. He doesn't hate a few others that he's friendly with."

"Stop!" Dad shouted. "I'm tired of all that crying for the colored. *No one* has it easy in this world."

Pauley went on as if he didn't even hear Dad. "Ed Jones hates white people for what they've done to his people. Once he told me a white man just

98

can't understand a black man. He just can't. Can we understand Arthur? He must have been afraid of Mr. Burke. I was. But I'll bet there was more to it than that. I'll bet Mr. Burke was thinking in his mind that Arthur was a little colored kid, a wise guy from over there in the ghetto, a kid who doesn't belong here anyway, a little nigger. So help me, I'm not exaggerating. I hear the colored kids talking and I know how we talk, us white kids. A day doesn't go by that we don't insult black people."

"Stop, kid, just stop. I don't want to hear any more of that." Dad yelled and pounded the table. Pauley went on repeating himself and repeating himself. Dad was mad, but at the very end he seemed to change his mind a little. I mean, he started smiling at Pauley while he talked. And he got up and got himself a beer and sat in his TV chair and leaned back a little and he listened with his eyes closed. Then he opened up and roared, "Stop!

"Hell, I know it's not fun being a colored man. If you're something else, Irish or Italian or German or Jewish or all that, you can mix with everyone else, at least you can a lot easier than the colored can. I'll give them a break—but not the whole cake, and not without work. They want too much too fast, and they want everything free, for nothing, just because they've suffered. We've *all* suffered."

Dad took a drink of his beer, and Pauley asked him please, *please* to stop using words like "nigger" and "colored." Dad got red again and yelled that he'd say what he damn well wanted to say, and Pauley had better listen.

"There were the potato famines in Ireland, and the Italians nearly starved to death, and that's why they came here. And the Jews, they've been pushed all over, and a lot of people don't like them, either. But instead of bellyaching and rioting and all that, and worrying what to call themselves, they tried to better themselves. If the colored worked more, got off welfare and *worked*, then they'd get ahead, and be more respected. That's how I see it. You can't just command respect in this world, or agitate to get it, or get it from a judge. Respect has to be earned, that's what I believe."

Dad stopped for a second and stared out the window. I thought he might be through talking, but no, he wasn't. "You and I are never going to agree on this. Why should we keep on fighting over the same thing? You'll have your chance. You'll have your kids. Go and tell them something different if you want to. But you'll be dead wrong if you fill them up with a lot of talk about 'equality' without telling what they're like, a lot of the colored."

Then Pauley lost his temper, the worst I've ever seen him do. He stood up and he said, "I'm tired of being treated like a child. I'm tired of you smiling at me while I talk, as if I'm a little kid."

Then he raised his voice and said it, he actually said it: "I'm not Marjie. I'm grown up and my mind is as good as yours, and I don't see why you should pat me on the head like a puppy. I'm sure of one thing. A lot of the people on this street treat their dogs better than they'd treat Arthur or any other black kid. You always tell us we've got to be good to Marjie because she's going to be up against a lot in her life. Well, so is Arthur. He's up against a lot, too."

Then Dad got up and knocked over his beer and I was scared he was going to hit Pauley. Pauley glared right at Dad and wouldn't move. Dad kept on going across the room toward Pauley. Mother came running in and stood between the two of them right in the nick of time.

"It's a good thing Marjie is not here to hear both of you. It's a good thing she's outside playing." She really screamed at Pauley. She called him a disgrace to the family. Then she turned around and shouted at Dad, too. "It's not only Pauley's fault. You should stop saying some of those things and leave the kids alone. If they don't agree with you, you have only yourself to blame. You've been telling that son of yours all his life that the next Paul Reynolds—*him*, your boy—would be a big man. He'd go to college and become a lawyer or something. Well, he's going to go. He's done all you've told him to do. He's read and read and he'll get a scholarship, they tell us. And the more he reads, the more ideas he gets about Freedom this and Freedom that and the poor colored people and the poor poor. Then he comes home and tells me that we're not poor. Well, someday he'll think twice about *that*, and he'll appreciate how hard it's been for his fa-

ther and his mother. There's no one bleeding his heart out for *us*! But until that day comes, I don't want any more fights here. No more! For Marjie's sake and mine and Andy's and David's."

She stopped and caught her breath and there were tears in her eyes. I thought she might be finished talking—but no, she had more to say: "The two of you have got to stop. I'm sick and tired of these fights. Do we have to have those demonstrators and all their talk come right into our house? Do we have to fight them, the colored and their fancy, rich supporters, right in our living room?"

Then she moved closer to Dad and she lowered her voice some. "Paul, you swore when we first got married that you'd keep a lot of what you saw while on duty away from my ears and the children's. Please remember that!"

Next she turned to my brother. "And you, Pauley, I won't have another word from you on this subject. Go and talk with your friends as you like. This is our home, and we're entitled to quiet here. We need it and we're going to have it. Now come and eat your supper."

IV

ARTHUR did come back to school after about a week, and so did Thomas. But before they came back we had a lot more trouble. Every day they'd be there picketing—the colored people and a lot of white people, too. And every day the police would be there. My dad told the lieutenant that because of me, he didn't want to be stationed at the school, and the lieutenant agreed. I overheard Dad telling Mom that the lieutenant said it was too *personal*—trying to protect a school your own kid is going to, and being insulted and called bad names in front of him.

For a day or two the school board thought of closing the school, but all the parents, including mine, went to a meeting and told the school people that if they did that—well, then they'd have *us* picketing, too. I didn't go to the meeting, but Mom told me that Dad stood up and said that the school is *ours,* and no one, absolutely no one, is going to take it away and force it to close down.

School kept going, and Mr. Burke kept on trying to ignore what was happening outside. He pretended everything was normal, the way it was before. And it began to seem longer and longer ago that he and Arthur had stood there in the aisle and he reached for Arthur and told him off. But one morning it all blew up in history.

Richey was reading out loud about Thomas Jefferson. The book said something about Jefferson having slaves but being against slavery and being sympathetic to colored people, even if he was from the South.

Richey did a good job and Mr. Burke told him so. Then Mr. Burke asked if any of us had any questions. No one raised a hand—except Richey himself. He asked Mr. Burke if he thought Thomas Jefferson would be as friendly to the colored people now as he was then. Mr. Burke said yes; he was sure Jefferson would feel the same now as he did then. I thought Richey asked a stupid question, because how can you tell what a man would think over a hundred years after he died? Mr. Burke was getting ready to call on someone else to read when Richey raised his hand again. Mr. Burke gave him a funny, impatient look and leaned back in his chair. Richey asked, "Would a man like Jefferson be in favor of what the colored people are doing now?"

Mr. Burke got red in the face, but he kept his temper. He just stared at Richey and said, "What do you have in mind?" Richey didn't answer. Mr. Burke asked him again, real slow and nasty, "What is it the colored people are doing that you want us to consider in the light of Thomas Jefferson's philosophy?"

That sure stumped Richey. He got red.

"Well, Richard," Mr. Burke said, after what seemed like an hour of silence, "you asked a question, but you can't spell out what you really want to know." And still not a word came from Richey—but he did glance out the window, and Mr. Burke saw him do it. We all did.

Mr. Burke suddenly got up. He walked toward the window and looked out. He opened the window, and we could hear someone yelling something against the school board and the police, but we couldn't make out every word. Then Mr. Burke shut the window hard, so hard I thought it would break. He walked over to his desk and pointed to the flag hanging beside it. For a second or two his mouth moved, but nothing came out. Finally the words came.

"This flag with all the stars on it, they didn't come here by accident. It took years and years, decades and decades, for this country to become the great nation that it is. We are the richest, strongest nation in the entire world. No country has ever been as great and powerful as this one. And we *are* a democracy. Men like Thomas Jefferson made sure that the American Revolution wasn't fought for no reason at all. They wanted the United States of America to be a solid, decent country, and they succeeded."

The words poured out and I got a shivery feeling, as if he were hitting us with them.

"But we can lose overnight what it took more

108

than a century to create. Thomas Jefferson believed in a government of laws and not in mob action. If he were alive today, if George Washington and John Adams and John Quincy Adams were alive today, they would be worried, as we all are, about violence in this nation. No group of people has the right to impose its wishes on another group. Changes must be lawful. It takes time for people to change their views. And you cannot force people to become different by threatening them and shouting at them and calling them names.''

He was raising his voice with every word. It was scary. Then one of the kids sitting in back of me—I didn't see who because it happened so fast—said, "Abraham Lincoln, what about him?"

Mr. Burke moved toward us and he pointed his ruler at us. "Abraham Lincoln freed the slaves. He did not say to them, take the whole country now, it's yours. There is a difference." And he slammed down the ruler on Richey's desk.

I was stuck to my seat I was so scared. But not the colored kids. They were as angry as Mr. Burke, and they were yelling at him and at each other. They stood up, *all four of them,* and they said they were going outside to be with their "brothers and sisters."

Mr. Burke had his mouth hanging down to his necktie. I don't think he believed what they were doing. As they moved toward the door, he dashed after them and said, "Return to your seats immediately or you'll be sent to Mr. Carter." They kept on moving around him, and he tried to push them back. As he grabbed at them they shifted and dodged around him like lightning, opened the door and ran. Mr. Burke walked to the window and just stood there. He must have seen them leaving the building, because he turned away suddenly and told us to stay in our seats and keep quiet and take out our books and read. He had to go and see the principal.

As soon as he left the room we all got up and crowded around the window. We heard a lot of noise out there, more than we'd ever heard before. We heard shouting. We heard: "Mr. Burke is a racist! He's got to go now. He's got to go." The kids from our room were talking to the demonstrators, and there were police standing right in front of the steps. Their clubs were out.

The sergeant was out front yelling, "Please, please stay on the sidewalk." But the demonstrators paid no attention. The policemen were standing stiff, just waiting for trouble. One walked to the squad car and leaned over to use the radio. "They'll be here in a minute," I told Richey, "about a dozen squad cars, you just wait and see."

They came, too—a lot of police cars and then the head of the school board and other people. The television people arrived, and we were back where we started, except that this time the police didn't let anyone get inside the school.

We all stood there, pushing at each other for a look out the window, or standing on the seats. Miss Knowlton came in and the kids stepped down. She didn't say much. She was white and shaky and she practically whispered that we should "take care" and not be "loud." Then she left, and we got back up on the seats.

I saw Mr. Carter come out of the building and go across the street. He stood there for a long time with some official-looking people and the police lieutenant.

"He's telling them to arrest the pickets," said the boy beside me. "If they arrest the pickets it won't do any good. More will come and there will be more trouble."

"The police can't go and arrest people unless there's a reason," I said. The police were caught in the middle, between the colored people and the school people, and it was a hard job, trying to do the right thing.

Richey said, "He was wrong. Mr. Burke was wrong to say what he did in front of the colored kids."

"What did he say that was so bad?" asked a girl named Shirley.

"Well, you can tell how he feels. Mr. Burke's against the colored people."

"You're crazy, Richey. Mr. Burke plays no favorites. He's mean but he's fair. My sister had him a few years ago, and I told her about all this business, and she said Mr. Burke screamed at her plenty, plenty!"

"O.K., Shirley, O.K.," said Richey. "But I bet there weren't any colored kids in her class!"

"My brother Pauley said there weren't any colored kids in the whole school. Maybe Mr. Burke never had any colored kids until this year. So how could *anyone* know how he's going to treat them—we're the ones who see him and hear what he says."

Shirley got real sore at Richey and me. "You two, you each just say what the other one does. My mother said they're all pushing on us, the niggers. They come up here from the South, and we've got to support them. They don't work. They're lazy. And a lot of them go running for help to the communists and the crazy hippies from the colleges."

"Oh, shut up Shirley," said her own friend Sally. Sally is no great talker. She's one of the quietest kids in the class.

"I will not shut up!"

"Well, you should. You're not talking sense."

"You said it, Sally," I shouted as loud as I could, and so did Richey and a lot of kids. Sally blushed.

Shirley saw she was on the losing side. "Forget it," she said. "I'm tired of all this. Why don't they all just come back—Arthur and Thomas and the other colored kids. One of the teachers said that's what'll happen."

"Don't wait for it," I said. "They won't come back. Would you?"

"I'm not a nigger," said Shirley. For a second I hated her, I wanted to hit her. Maybe I would have, but just then Miss Knowlton came in and told us we were making too much noise. She had us all sit down and she told us to stay down, and she meant *stay*. She kept looking in on us, and she kept telling us to stay *put* and stay *quiet* and stay *still*—until finally she came and surprised us and said, "Get up, all of you, and go to your lunch."

When we came back, guess who was waiting for us? Mr. Carter and the colored kids were there. Not Arthur and Thomas, but the four who ran out earlier in the day.

"I have something to tell this class," Mr. Carter said as soon as we got to our seats, and that was a lot faster than usual. "Mr. Burke is not feeling well, and I've told him to go home for the day. We will have a substitute teacher, a very good one, for you in an hour or so. Meanwhile I'll stay with you." We all looked around at each other and someone groaned. "Your two classmates, the two boys who left this room so suddenly a week or so ago, will be back tomorrow. Their mothers have assured me that will be the case."

We did get a substitute, a nice lady named Mrs. Ellis, and they did come back, Arthur and Thomas, just as Mr. Carter said they would. They didn't want to talk much, and we didn't know what to say to them. Richey was the first one in the class to say *anything* to them. He went up and said, "Welcome back," and they nodded, that's all. I tried to talk with Arthur and he wouldn't answer me. Thomas and I used to talk a little, and I believe if we hadn't gone through all that trouble maybe Thomas and I could have been friends. We're both good at baseball, and he likes to laugh. Arthur is always serious. But Arthur and Thomas have been like twins ever since they returned, sticking together like glue. Sometimes I see Thomas watching us, especially on the playground. But he sticks with Arthur and Arthur sticks with him—and they don't have much to do with us.

On television they said the school was "back to normal." There had been an agreement, but they never did tell us what the agreement was. The papers said that the school people had promised the Negro people that their kids would be "treated fairly, like all other children." Mr. Carter had promised so, and the superintendent said on the TV news that Mr. Burke hadn't been feeling well, and he had requested a "change of duties."

"They kicked poor old Burke upstairs," said my dad. "He won't be assistant principal like they say on TV and in the papers. He'll be an office helper until things quiet down. They'll keep the Negro kids and Mr. Burke away from each other for a few weeks, maybe until the end of the school year. It's face-saving, Andy. That's what it is. Everyone is doing it, saving face. In this world people fight to win or lose. When they're evenly matched, they both have to give ground. The colored people knew they could only keep their picketing going so long, because eventually everyone gets tired, even the picketers themselves. The school people wanted to settle, because it looks bad on their record—Mr. Carter's and Mr. Burke's and the superintendent's. Then you have a lot of the rich people and do-gooders agitating for the colored, pressuring the school officials. And I'm tired of being in the middle. Someone has got to understand how a man like me feels, to see the problems *we* have in this neighborhood. People have got to respect the law."

Dad was on duty that night. Mom had pressed his uniform and he was getting ready to leave. Pauley was still at it. "They came here, the Negroes, and did all that work and never got a cent because they were slaves. Now they want to be free and make a living, and if that happens, it'll be better for everyone. We'll all have more freedom and black people won't be a burden on white people and white people won't be a burden on black people."

"No more sermons, Pauley," Dad said. "Stop those lectures. That's all I hear these days. Let's forget the whole business, at least for one day! Let's wait and see what happens in Andy's school. But we're not turning this house into a battlefield. It's all too much for me."

He stood there in front of the door, tired but ready to go in his uniform, and I felt sorry for him. Because I knew we would always be arguing. But we are a family. He kissed Marjie goodnight, and Mom hugged him. Then he was gone.

P1